This book belongs to:

_____

Thanks to my Mom, for introducing me to Emily Carr at an impressionable young age. And to my Grandma, who not-so-secretly wanted me to be a scientist, but was always proud of me anyway.

Tundra Books, an imprint of Penguin Random House Canada Young Readers, a Penguin Random House Company

Library and Archives Canada Cataloguing in Publication

Title: When Emily was small / Lauren Soloy.
Names: Soloy, Lauren, author.
Identifiers: Canadiana (print) 2019015831X | Canadiana (ebook) 20190158336 | ISBN 9780735266063
  (hardcover) | ISBN 9780735266070 (EPUB)
Subjects: LCSH: Carr, Emily, 1871-1945-Juvenile fiction.
Classification: LCC PS8637.O4472 W44 2020 | DDC jC813/.6-dc23

Published simultaneously in the United States of America by Tundra Books of Northern New York, an imprint of Penguin Random House Canada Young Readers, a Penguin Random House Company

Library of Congress Control Number: 2019946660

Edited by Samantha Swenson
Designed by Emma Dolan
The artwork in this book was rendered in watercolors, pencils, crayons, pastels, gouache, papers, ink and pixels using brushes, scissors, glue sticks and love.
The text was set in Carrotflower and KG Fall For You.

Printed and bound in China

www.penguinrandomhouse.ca

1   2   3   4   5   24   23   22   21   20

Penguin
Random House
TUNDRA BOOKS

When Emily was Small

Lauren Soloy

tundra

Once there was a girl who would
grow up to be the artist Emily Carr.

But this is a story about
when she was small.

Emily's feet danced her, lippity-lippety,
through her father's vegetable garden.

"Hello," she said to the beans,
"Hello," to the sun-sparkled leaves.
"Hello, cabbages; hello, breeze."

She slipped through the currant bushes —
past the purple and red — and into . . .

Her favorite — the white currants.
Clusters of ripe berries glowed
in the sunlight. Emily studied one,
looking past translucent skin to
veins and juice and seeds within.
There was a glitter-glimmer at the
heart of it that stayed hidden . . .

no matter how closely she looked.
"Hello, secret," she said.

Then she crawled past the currant
bushes to the spare place beside the
fence, where the garden scraps were
dumped. Weeds and wildflowers
grew there, higgledy-piggledy.

"Hello, wild place," Emily said.
It answered her with a sweet
pink smell that called to bees
and butterflies and other
trembly things.

Emily sat and cleared her mind.

She listened to the cow lowing
in the cow yard and the ducks
quacking on the pond. Distantly,
she could hear the mighty roar
of the waves crashing against
the shore, then slipping away
in small but ceaseless sighs.

For a moment, she was filled
with peace.

Then, out of the shimmering stillness, in the space between one heartbeat and the next—

Thumpety . . .

Bumpety, the silence was filled with presence.

"Hello," said the Wild.
"Who are you?"

"Hello, Wild," she said.
"I am Small."

The Wild grabbed her hand
with toothy glee.

"Hello, Small. There is so
much to show you!"

"Look and see how the color you think of as green
is really a thousand shades and hues."

"See how sunlight glows
in every shadow."

The Wild and Small were surrounded by sun-dazzled wings, flickering among clouds of flowers.

A hum and buzz rose all around them then, swishing and shushing and gushing and hushing.

"Hello, glow!"
sang Small.

"Hello, bee!"

"Hello, blossoms,
fizzing with glee!"

"But most of all," said the Wild, "Small..."

"You are Bigger than you know!"

And then they flew. They flew so
fast and so high that the leaves and
petals and wings all blurred into one
lovely thing. The restless seas and
towering trees sang a deep and
vast song, like a wild beating
heart of now.

Thumpety-Bumpety. Thumpety...

Bump.

Suddenly, all was still.
Small and the Wild were
suspended in the center of it
all, like seeds in a currant.

Everything around them
hummed and thrummed
with life.

And behind it all . . .

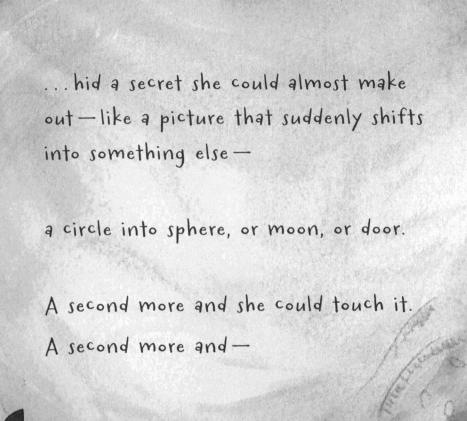

...hid a secret she could almost make
out—like a picture that suddenly shifts
into something else—

a circle into sphere, or moon, or door.

A second more and she could touch it.
A second more and—

"Emily! You're covered in dirt!"

The Wild vanished. The leaves and petals and bees became themselves again.

Emily's mother brushed off the dirt
and greenery that clung to Emily's
dress, making it respectable and plain,
and Emily felt herself shrink back
down to become small once more.

And yet, looking back, she couldn't help
but notice the butterfly's wings . . .

...dancing to the rhythm of her own
small heart, drumming gaily in her chest.

Thumpety-Bumpety. Thumpety...

Bump.

Emily Carr is mostly known for her paintings —
scenes of West Coast wilderness and Indigenous cultures
— but it wasn't always that way. She often felt alone and
unappreciated as she struggled to make ends meet. It was only
later in her life, when her association with the painting group
known as the Group of Seven developed, that people began
to appreciate her unique vision. In her day, she was better
known for her autobiographical writing. This book is based
on the story "White Currants" from her book THE BOOK OF
SMALL. It offers a glimpse into the childhood of one
of our greatest artists — of a time when she thought of
herself as "Small" more often than as Emily.

Emily Carr was someone who strove her whole life to
experience the bigness of things. She looked everywhere for
the secret behind the beauty, and not only did she attempt
to see it, she tried always to share that mystery with the
rest of us. I am so grateful that she did.